# JUST BEYOND ™

## VOLUME 5:
## THE HORROR
## AT HAPPY LANDINGS

Written by
### R.L. Stine

Illustrated by
### Kelly & Nichole Matthews

Lettered by
**Mike Fiorentino**

Cover by
**Julian Totino Tedesco**

*Just Beyond* created by
**R.L. Stine**

Designer
**Scott Newman**

Assistant Editor
**Michael Moccio**

Associate Editor
**Sophie Philips-Roberts**

Editor
**Bryce Carlson**

 Spotlig

**ABDOBOOKS.COM**

Reinforced library bound edition published in 2021 by Spotlight, a division of ABDO, PO Box 398166, Minneapolis, Minnesota 55439. Spotlight produces high-quality reinforced library bound editions for schools and libraries.
Published by agreement with KaBOOM!

Printed in the United States of America, North Mankato, Minnesota.
092020
012021

THIS BOOK CONTAINS RECYCLED MATERIALS

kaboom!™



BOOM! Studios, 5670 Wilshire Boulevard, Suite 400, Los Angeles, CA 90036-5679.

Library of Congress Control Number: 2020940819

Publisher's Cataloging-in-Publication Data

Names: Stine, R.L., author. | Matthews, Kelly; Matthews, Nichole, illustrators.
Title: The horror at happy landings / by R.L. Stine; illustrated by Kelly Matthews, and Nichole Matthews.
Description: Minneapolis, Minnesota : Spotlight, 2021. | Series: Just beyond; volume 5
Summary: Family camping trips are supposed to be fun, but for Parker, Annie, and the Walden family, their trip turns into a nightmare when Parker and Annie get stuck in a swarm of bees, and their mom is attacked by a Martian bird, which belongs to two stranded aliens trying to find their way home.
Identifiers: ISBN 9781532147555 (lib. bdg.)
Subjects: LCSH: Camping--Juvenile fiction. | Families--Juvenile fiction. | Bees--Juvenile fiction. | Extraterrestrial beings--Juvenile fiction. | Animal attacks--Juvenile fiction. | Adventure stories--Juvenile fiction. | Graphic Novels--Juvenile fiction. | Comic books, strips, etc.--Juvenile fiction.
Classification: DDC 741.5--dc23

ABDO
**Spotlight**

A Division of ABDO
abdobooks.com

# CHAPTER ONE
# THE SWARM

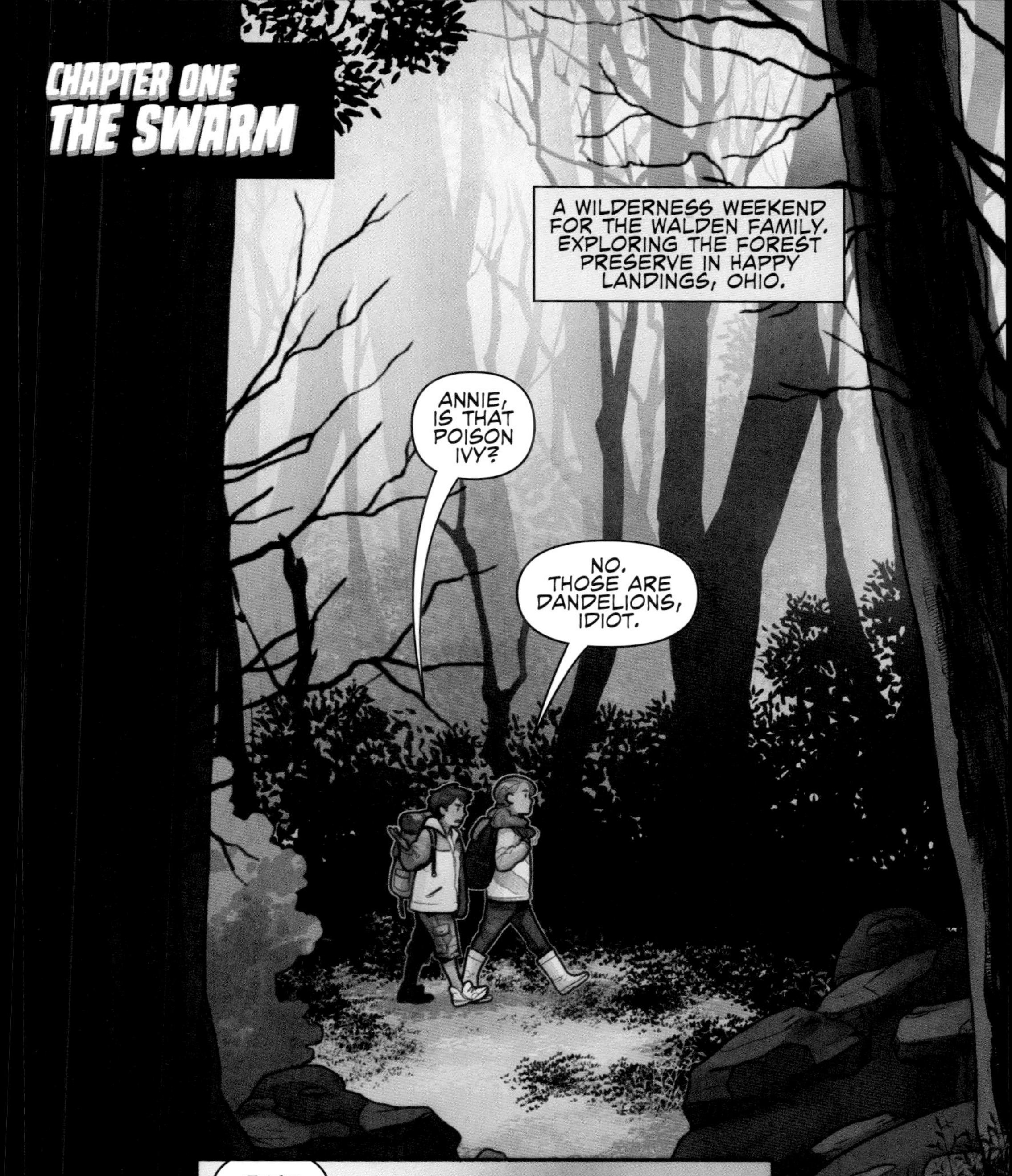
A WILDERNESS WEEKEND FOR THE WALDEN FAMILY. EXPLORING THE FOREST PRESERVE IN HAPPY LANDINGS, OHIO.
ANNIE, IS THAT POISON IVY?
NO. THOSE ARE DANDELIONS, IDIOT.

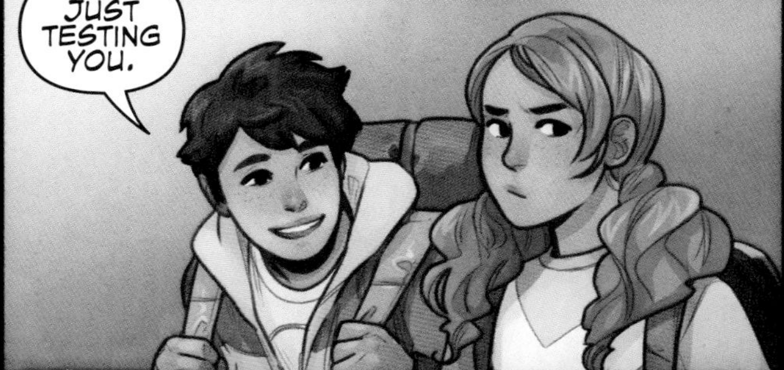
JUST TESTING YOU.

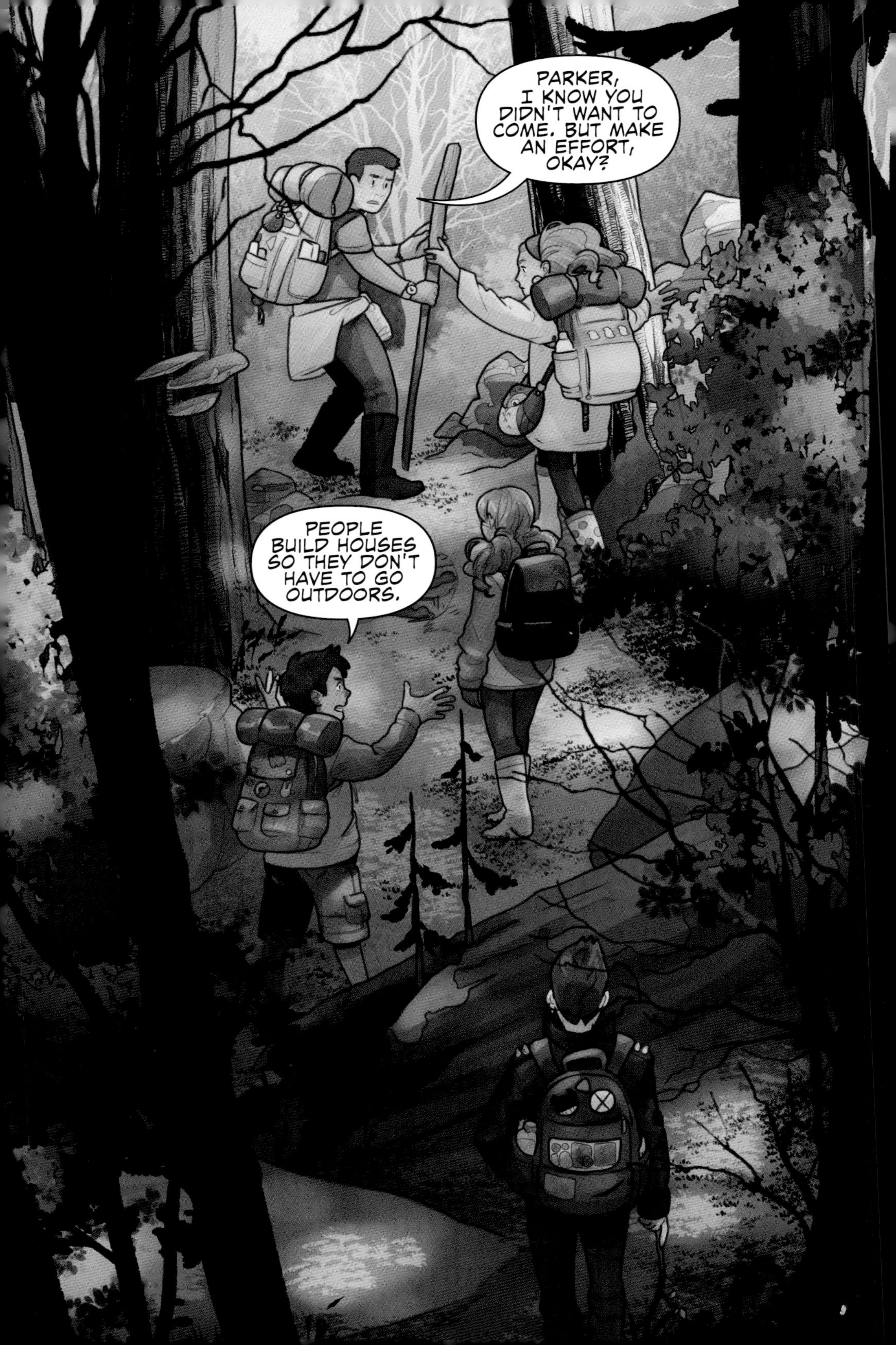
PARKER, I KNOW YOU DIDN'T WANT TO COME. BUT MAKE AN EFFORT, OKAY?
PEOPLE BUILD HOUSES SO THEY DON'T HAVE TO GO OUTDOORS.

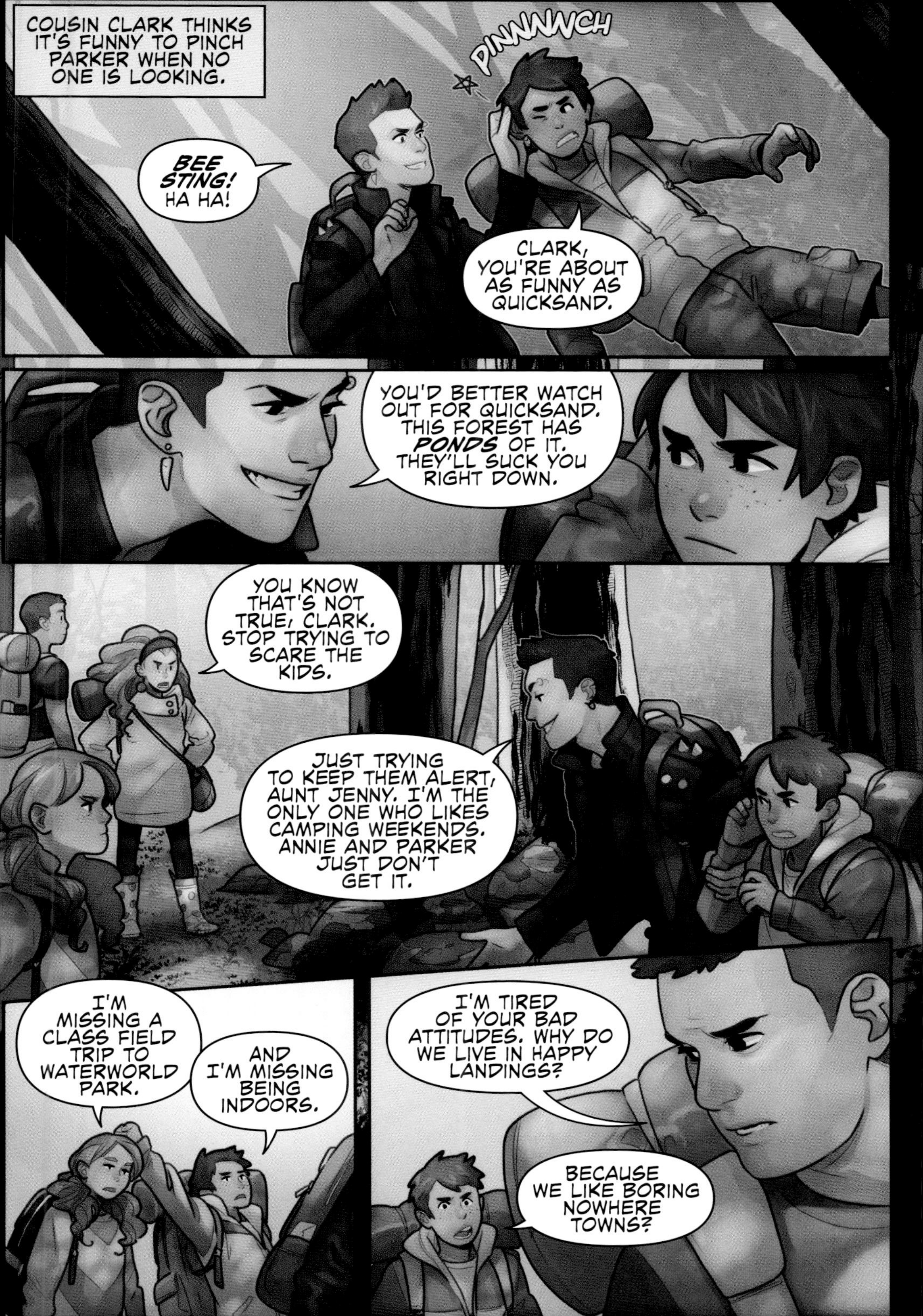
COUSIN CLARK THINKS IT'S FUNNY TO PINCH PARKER WHEN NO ONE IS LOOKING.
PINNNNCH
BEE STING! HA HA!
CLARK, YOU'RE ABOUT AS FUNNY AS QUICKSAND.
YOU'D BETTER WATCH OUT FOR QUICKSAND. THIS FOREST HAS PONDS OF IT. THEY'LL SUCK YOU RIGHT DOWN.
YOU KNOW THAT'S NOT TRUE, CLARK. STOP TRYING TO SCARE THE KIDS.
JUST TRYING TO KEEP THEM ALERT, AUNT JENNY. I'M THE ONLY ONE WHO LIKES CAMPING WEEKENDS. ANNIE AND PARKER JUST DON'T GET IT.
I'M MISSING A CLASS FIELD TRIP TO WATERWORLD PARK.
AND I'M MISSING BEING INDOORS.
I'M TIRED OF YOUR BAD ATTITUDES. WHY DO WE LIVE IN HAPPY LANDINGS?
BECAUSE WE LIKE BORING NOWHERE TOWNS?

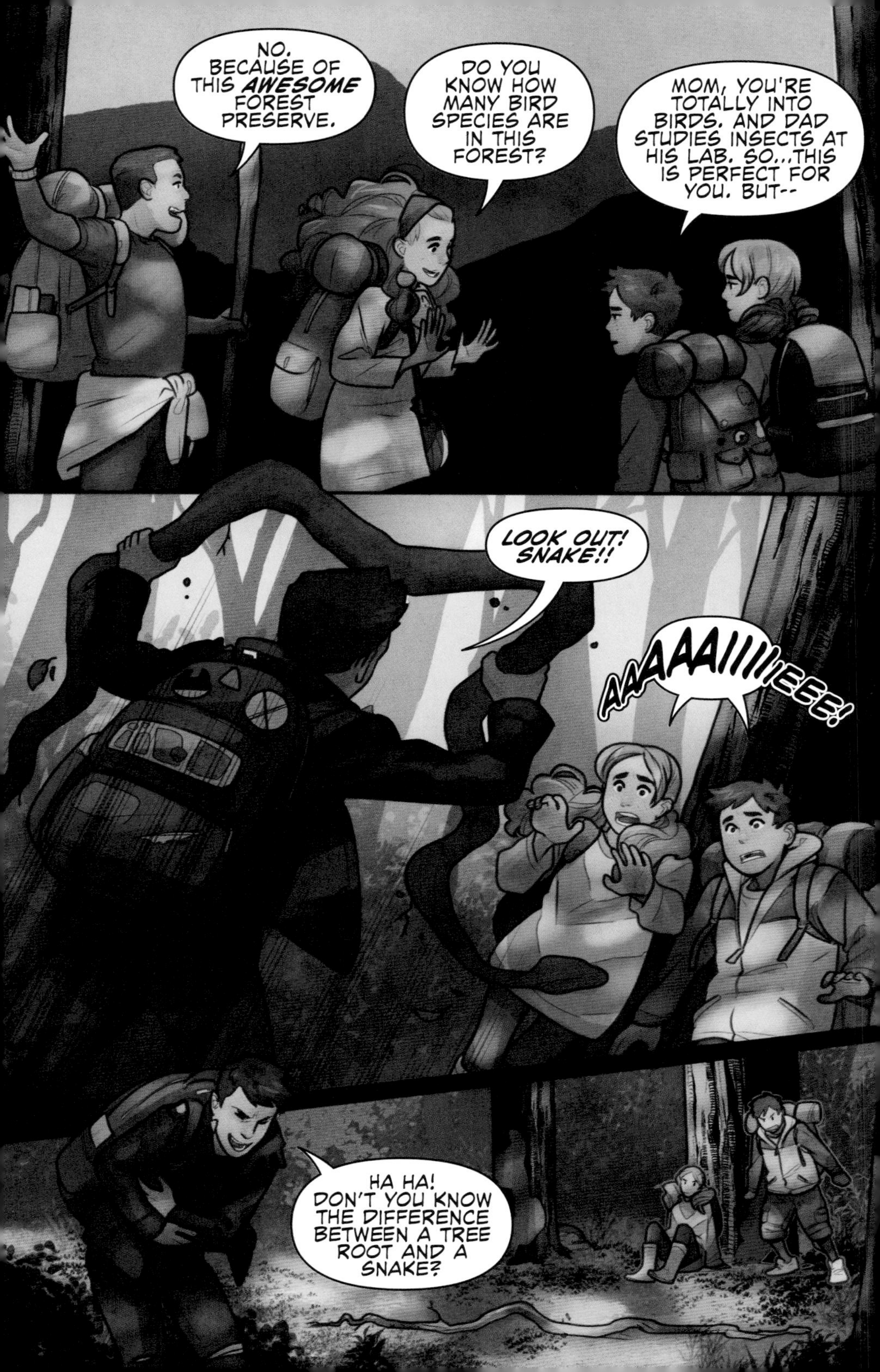
NO. BECAUSE OF THIS AWESOME FOREST PRESERVE.
DO YOU KNOW HOW MANY BIRD SPECIES ARE IN THIS FOREST?
MOM, YOU'RE TOTALLY INTO BIRDS. AND DAD STUDIES INSECTS AT HIS LAB. SO...THIS IS PERFECT FOR YOU. BUT--
LOOK OUT! SNAKE!!
AAAAAIIIIIIEEEE!
HA HA! DON'T YOU KNOW THE DIFFERENCE BETWEEN A TREE ROOT AND A SNAKE?

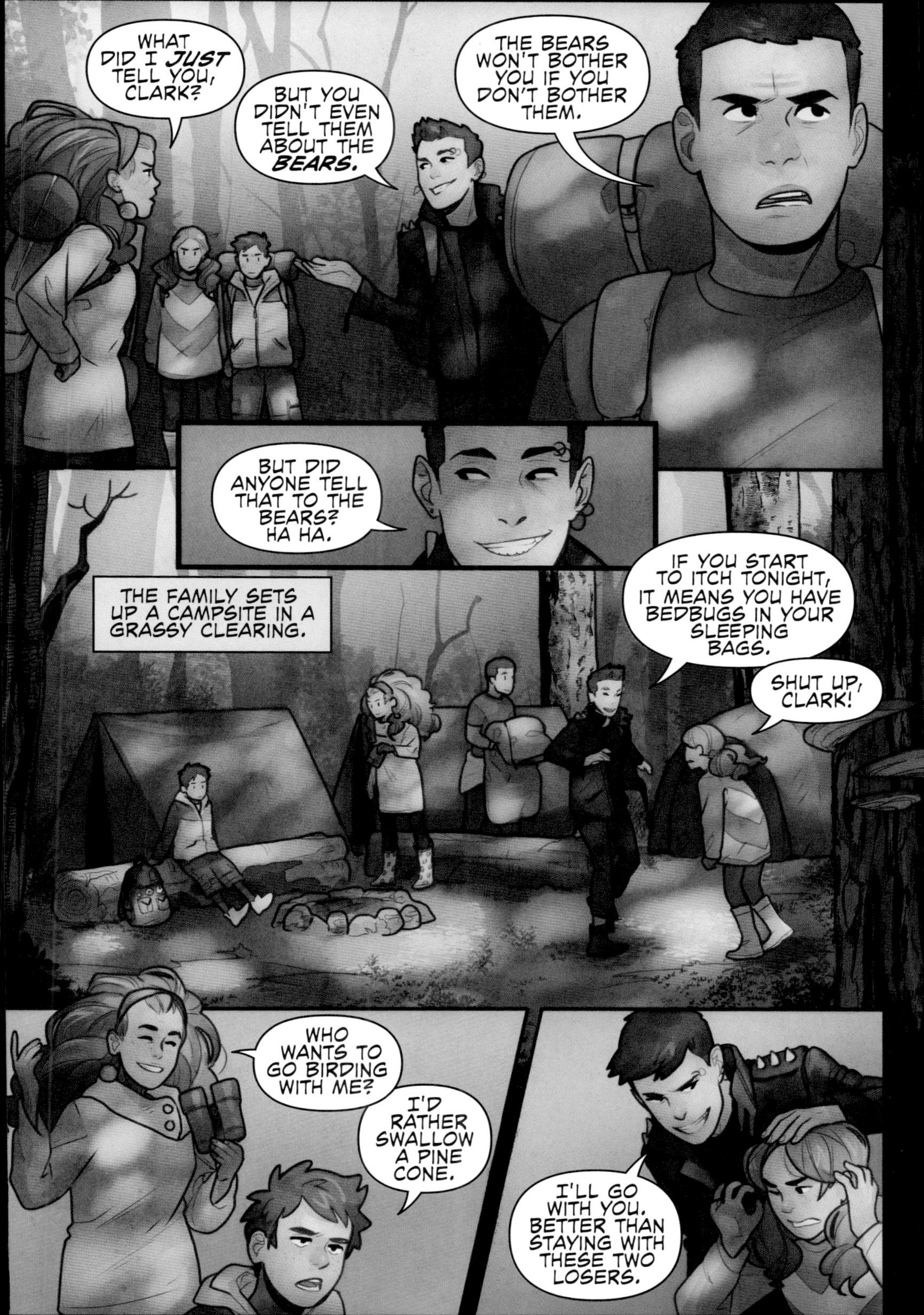

WHAT DID I *JUST* TELL YOU, CLARK?
BUT YOU DIDN'T EVEN TELL THEM ABOUT THE ***BEARS.***
THE BEARS WON'T BOTHER YOU IF YOU DON'T BOTHER THEM.
BUT DID ANYONE TELL THAT TO THE BEARS? HA HA.
THE FAMILY SETS UP A CAMPSITE IN A GRASSY CLEARING.
IF YOU START TO ITCH TONIGHT, IT MEANS YOU HAVE BEDBUGS IN YOUR SLEEPING BAGS.
SHUT UP, CLARK!
WHO WANTS TO GO BIRDING WITH ME?
I'D RATHER SWALLOW A PINE CONE.
I'LL GO WITH YOU. BETTER THAN STAYING WITH THESE TWO LOSERS.

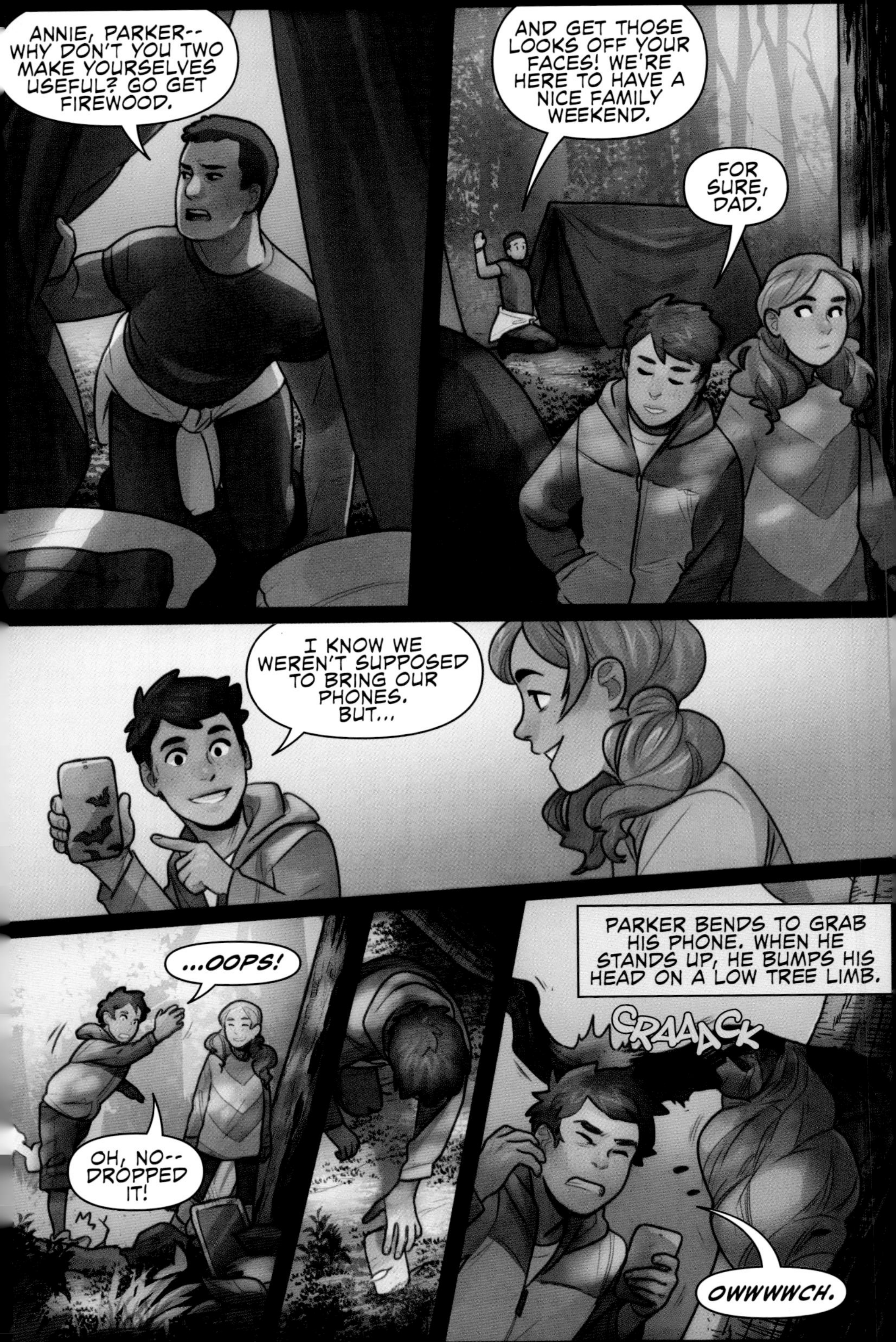
ANNIE, PARKER-- WHY DON'T YOU TWO MAKE YOURSELVES USEFUL? GO GET FIREWOOD.
AND GET THOSE LOOKS OFF YOUR FACES! WE'RE HERE TO HAVE A NICE FAMILY WEEKEND.
FOR SURE, DAD.
I KNOW WE WEREN'T SUPPOSED TO BRING OUR PHONES. BUT...
...OOPS!
OH, NO-- DROPPED IT!
PARKER BENDS TO GRAB HIS PHONE. WHEN HE STANDS UP, HE BUMPS HIS HEAD ON A LOW TREE LIMB.
CRAAACK
OWWWWCH.

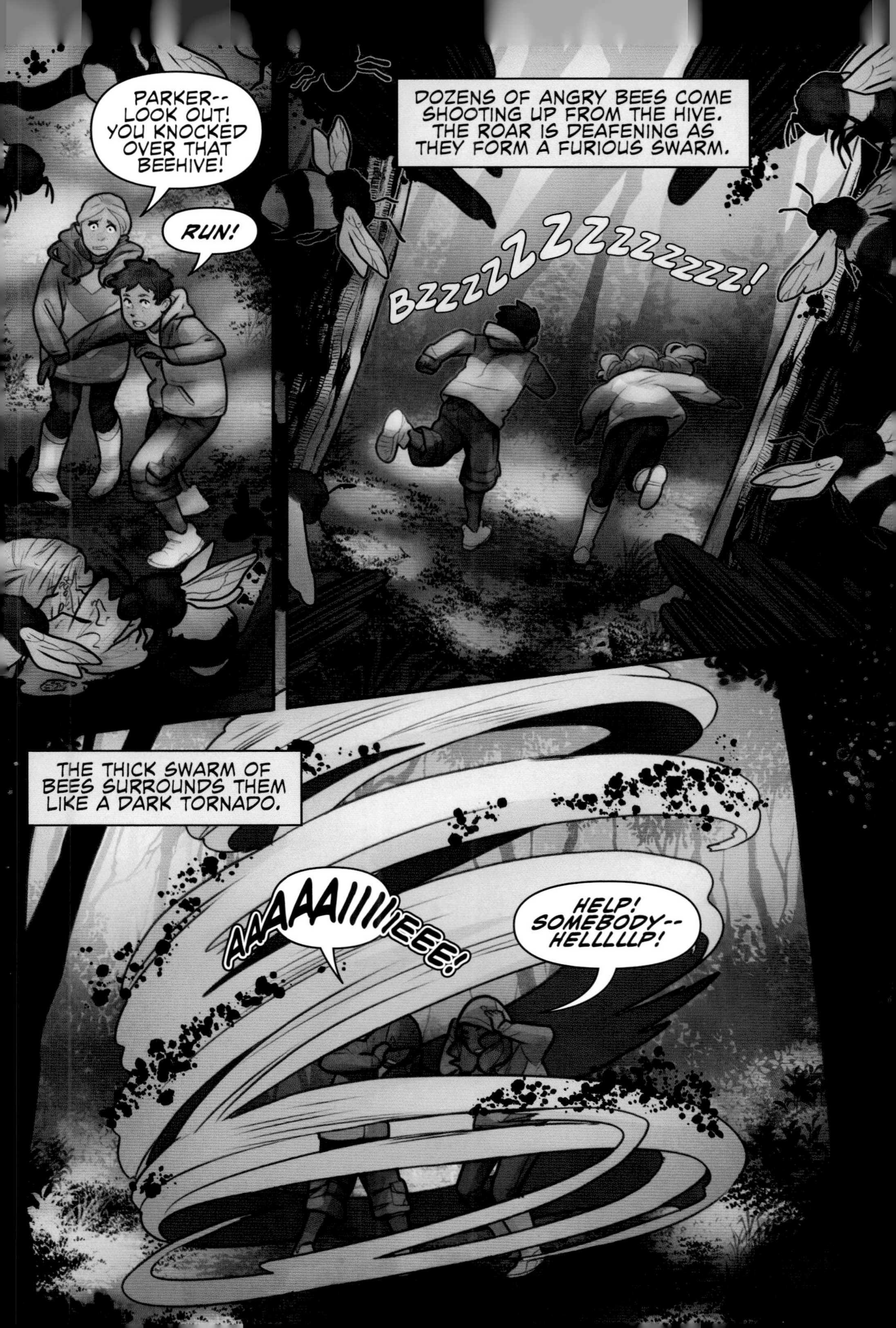
PARKER-- LOOK OUT! YOU KNOCKED OVER THAT BEEHIVE!
RUN!
DOZENS OF ANGRY BEES COME SHOOTING UP FROM THE HIVE. THE ROAR IS DEAFENING AS THEY FORM A FURIOUS SWARM.
BZZZZZZZZZZZZZZZ!
THE THICK SWARM OF BEES SURROUNDS THEM LIKE A DARK TORNADO.
AAAAAIIIIIIEEEE!
HELP! SOMEBODY-- HELLLLLP!

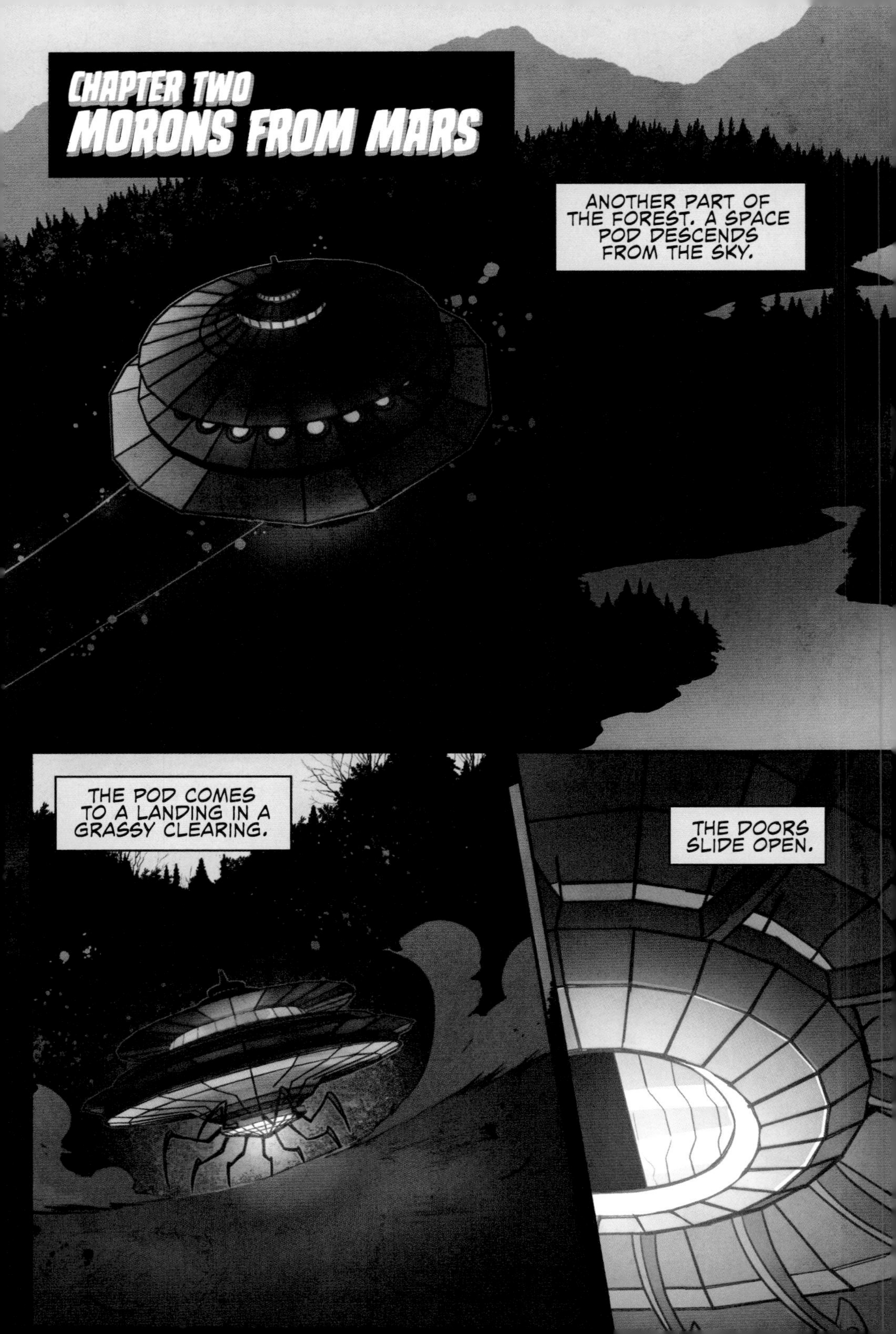
CHAPTER TWO
MORONS FROM MARS
ANOTHER PART OF THE FOREST. A SPACE POD DESCENDS FROM THE SKY.
THE POD COMES TO A LANDING IN A GRASSY CLEARING.
THE DOORS SLIDE OPEN.

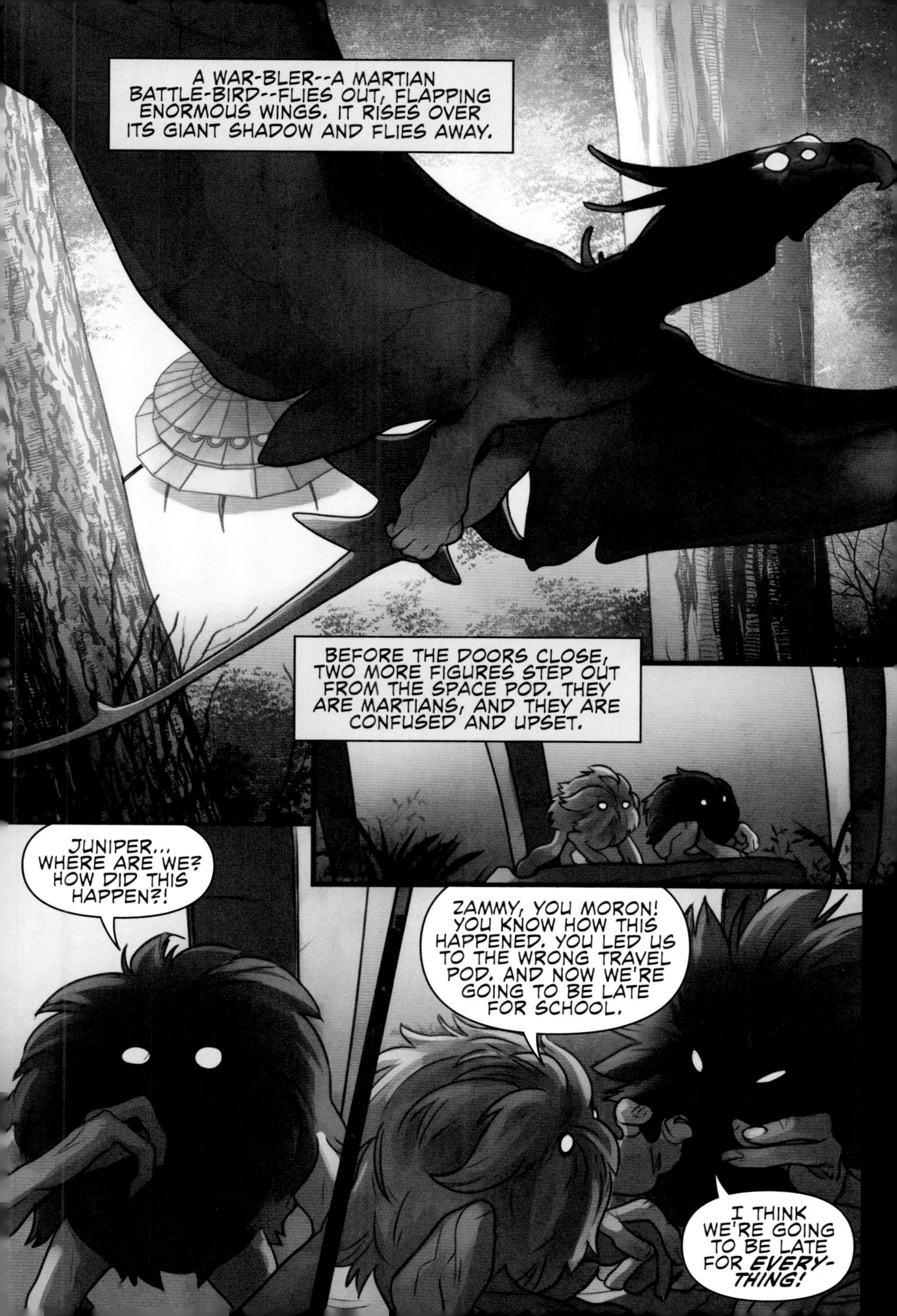
A WAR-BLER--A MARTIAN BATTLE-BIRD--FLIES OUT, FLAPPING ENORMOUS WINGS. IT RISES OVER ITS GIANT SHADOW AND FLIES AWAY.
BEFORE THE DOORS CLOSE, TWO MORE FIGURES STEP OUT FROM THE SPACE POD. THEY ARE MARTIANS, AND THEY ARE CONFUSED AND UPSET.
JUNIPER... WHERE ARE WE? HOW DID THIS HAPPEN?!
ZAMMY, YOU MORON! YOU KNOW HOW THIS HAPPENED. YOU LED US TO THE WRONG TRAVEL POD. AND NOW WE'RE GOING TO BE LATE FOR SCHOOL.
I THINK WE'RE GOING TO BE LATE FOR *EVERYTHING!*

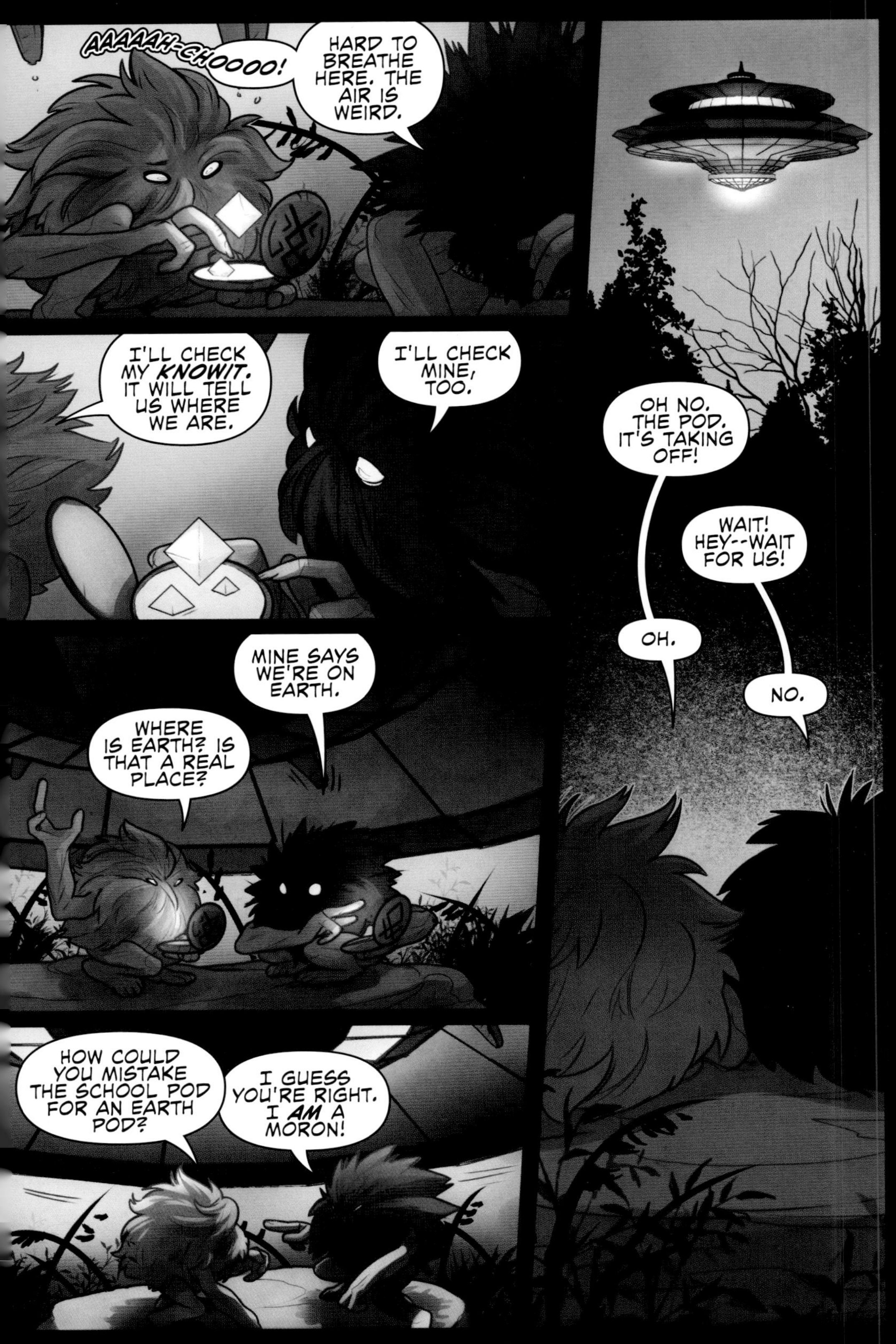
AAAAAH-CHOOOOO!
HARD TO BREATHE HERE. THE AIR IS WEIRD.
I'LL CHECK MY *KNOWIT.* IT WILL TELL US WHERE WE ARE.
I'LL CHECK MINE, TOO.
MINE SAYS WE'RE ON EARTH.
WHERE IS EARTH? IS THAT A REAL PLACE?
HOW COULD YOU MISTAKE THE SCHOOL POD FOR AN EARTH POD?
I GUESS YOU'RE RIGHT. I *AM* A MORON!
OH NO. THE POD. IT'S TAKING OFF!
WAIT! HEY--WAIT FOR US!
OH.
NO.

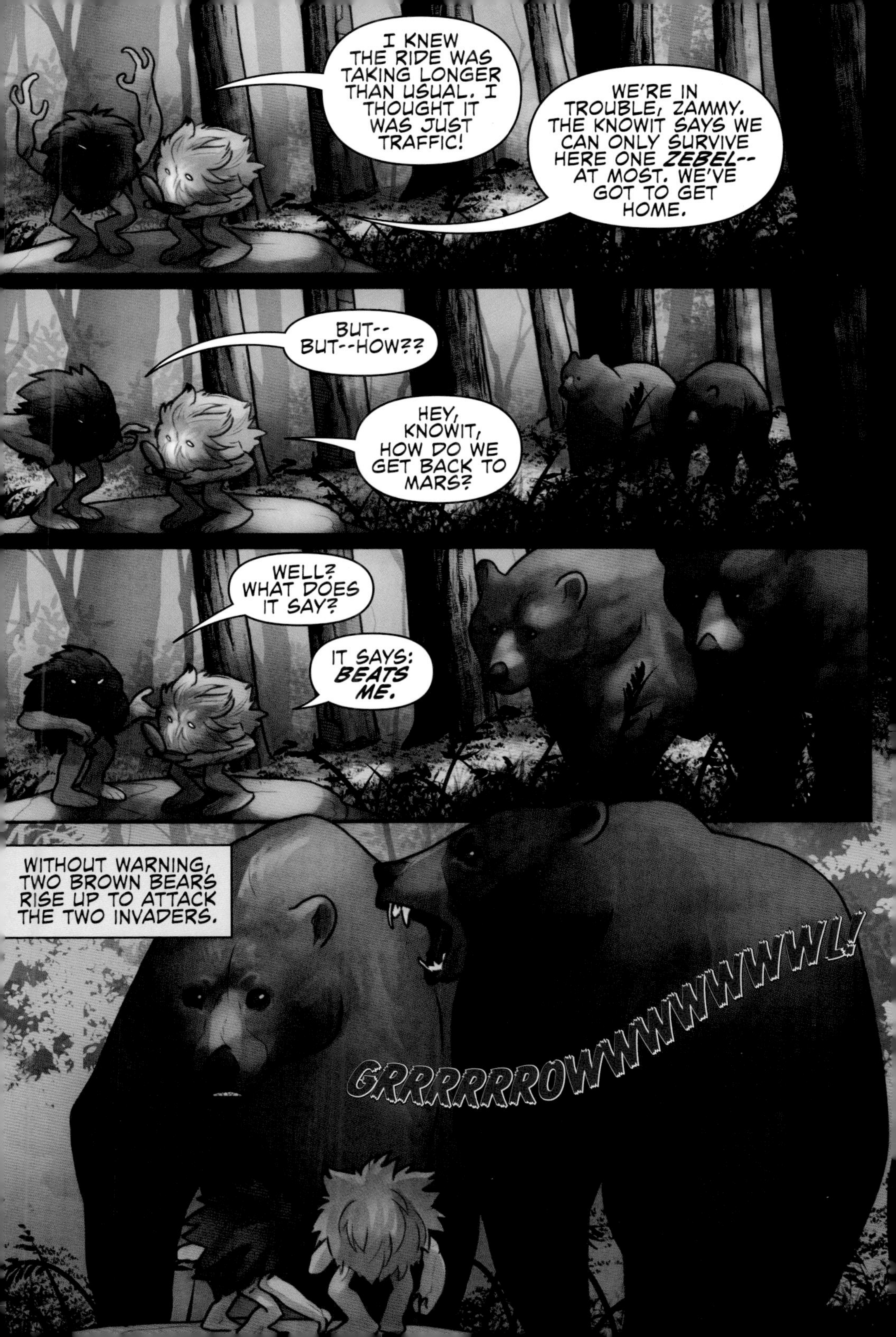
I KNEW THE RIDE WAS TAKING LONGER THAN USUAL. I THOUGHT IT WAS JUST TRAFFIC!
WE'RE IN TROUBLE, ZAMMY. THE KNOWIT SAYS WE CAN ONLY SURVIVE HERE ONE ZEBEL-- AT MOST. WE'VE GOT TO GET HOME.
BUT-- BUT--HOW??
HEY, KNOWIT, HOW DO WE GET BACK TO MARS?
WELL? WHAT DOES IT SAY?
IT SAYS: BEATS ME.
WITHOUT WARNING, TWO BROWN BEARS RISE UP TO ATTACK THE TWO INVADERS.
GRRRRRROWWWWWWWWL!

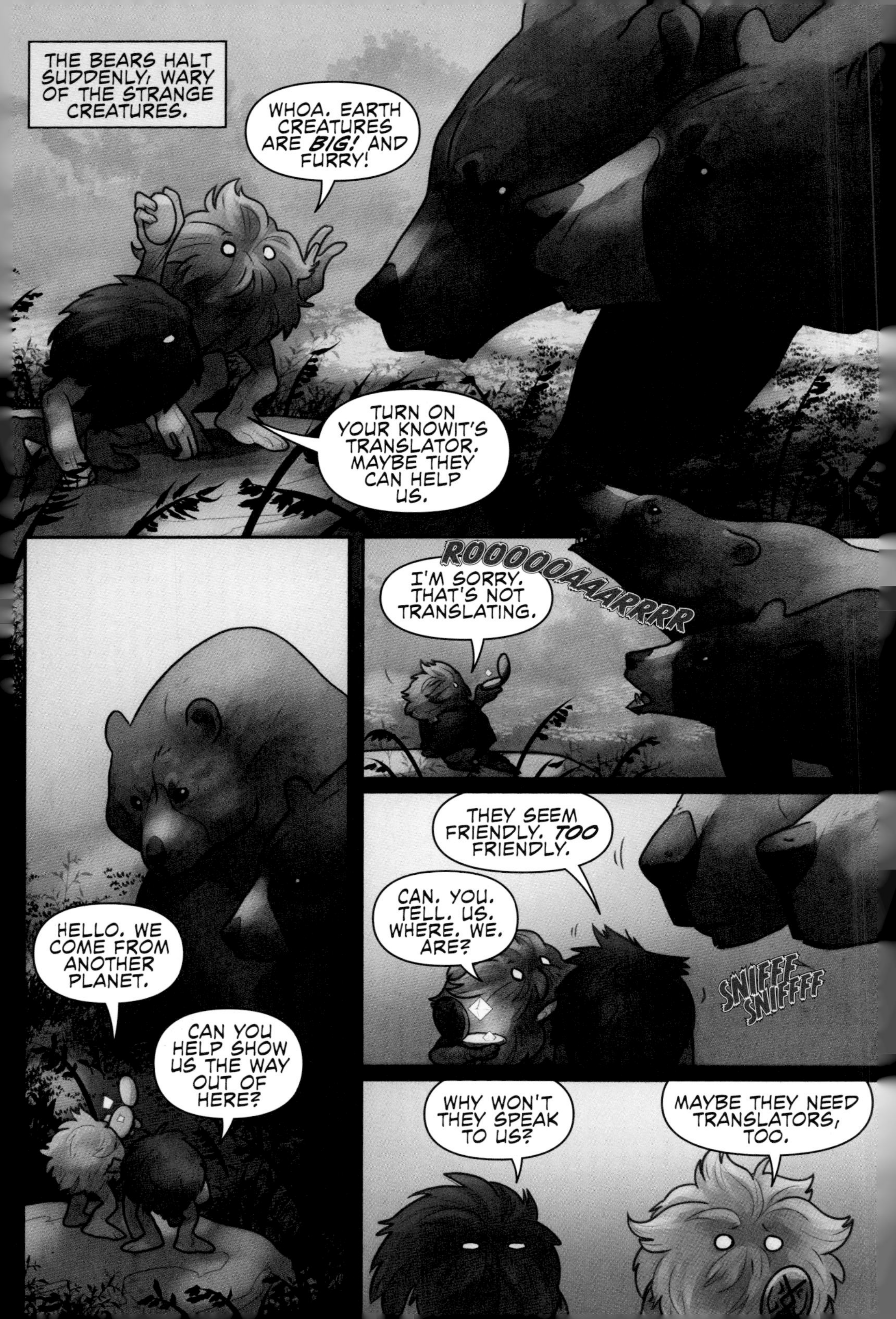
THE BEARS HALT SUDDENLY, WARY OF THE STRANGE CREATURES.
WHOA. EARTH CREATURES ARE *BIG!* AND FURRY!
TURN ON YOUR KNOWIT'S TRANSLATOR. MAYBE THEY CAN HELP US.
HELLO. WE COME FROM ANOTHER PLANET.
CAN YOU HELP SHOW US THE WAY OUT OF HERE?
ROOOOOOAAARRRR
I'M SORRY. THAT'S NOT TRANSLATING.
THEY SEEM FRIENDLY. *TOO* FRIENDLY.
CAN. YOU. TELL. US. WHERE. WE. ARE?
SNIFFF SNIFFFF
WHY WON'T THEY SPEAK TO US?
MAYBE THEY NEED TRANSLATORS, TOO.

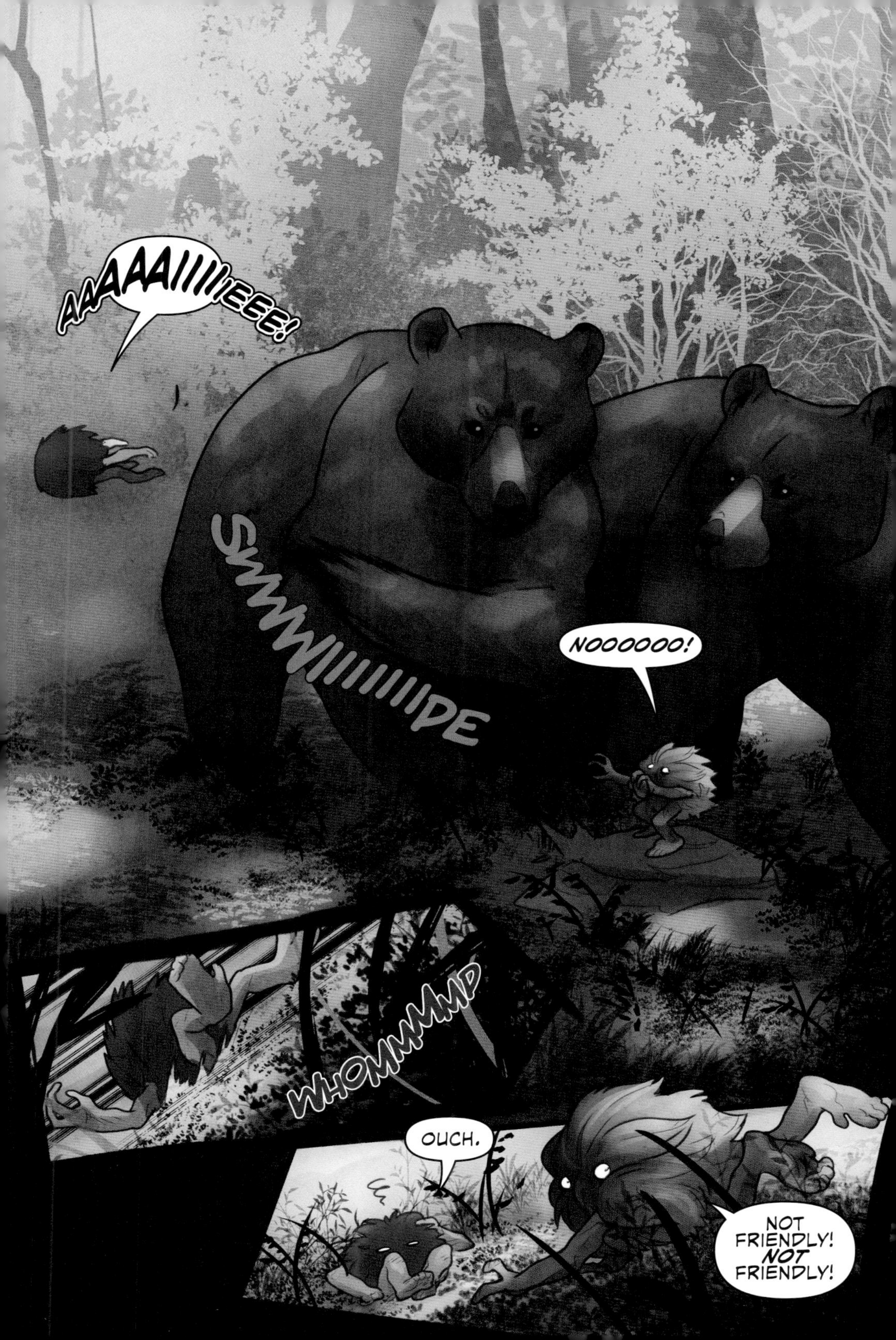
AAAAAIIIIIEEEE!
SWWWIIIIIIIIPE
NOOOOOO!
WHOMMMMMP
OUCH.
NOT FRIENDLY! *NOT* FRIENDLY!

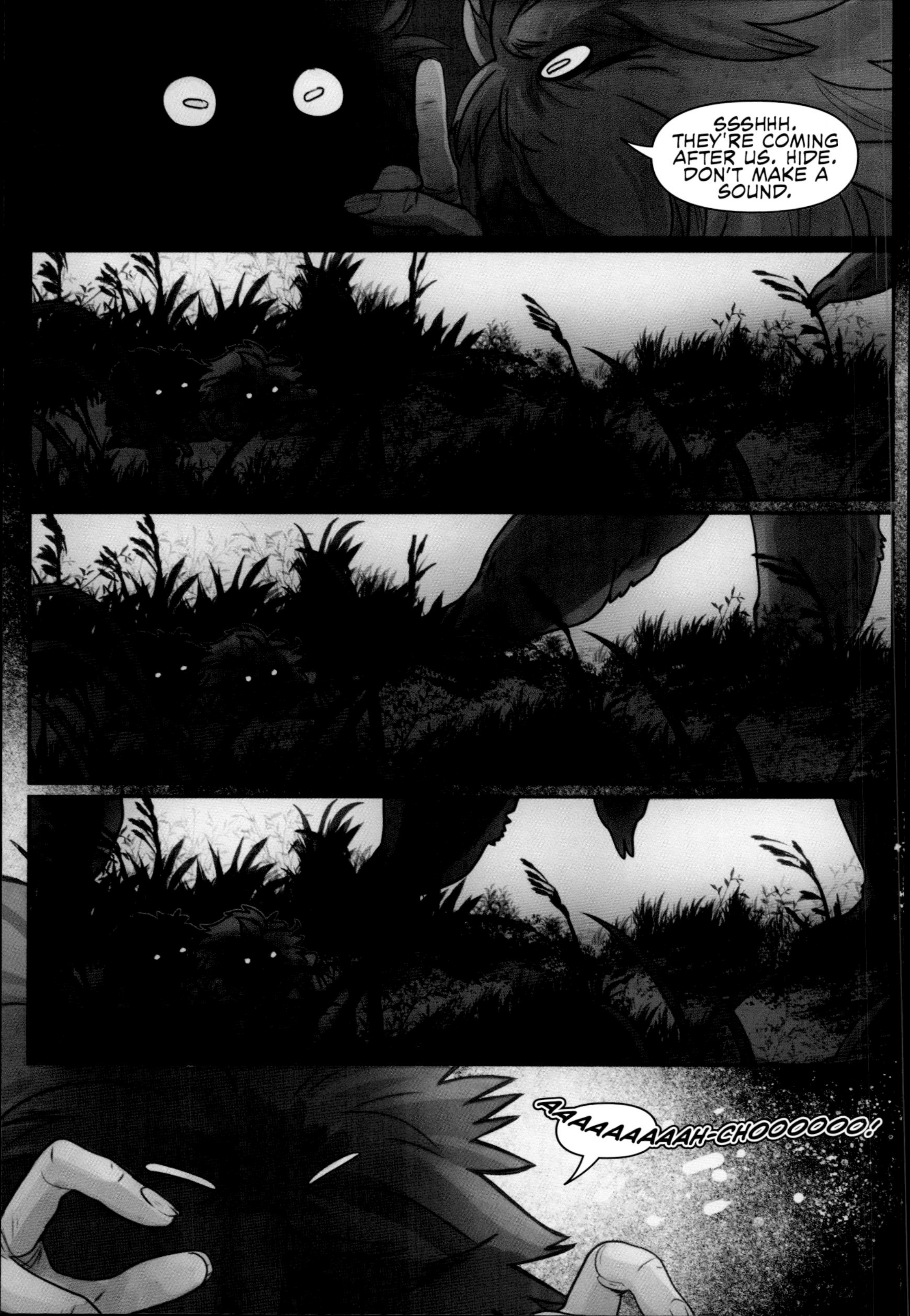
SSSHHH. THEY'RE COMING AFTER US. HIDE. DON'T MAKE A SOUND.
AAAAAAAAAH-CHOOOOOOO!

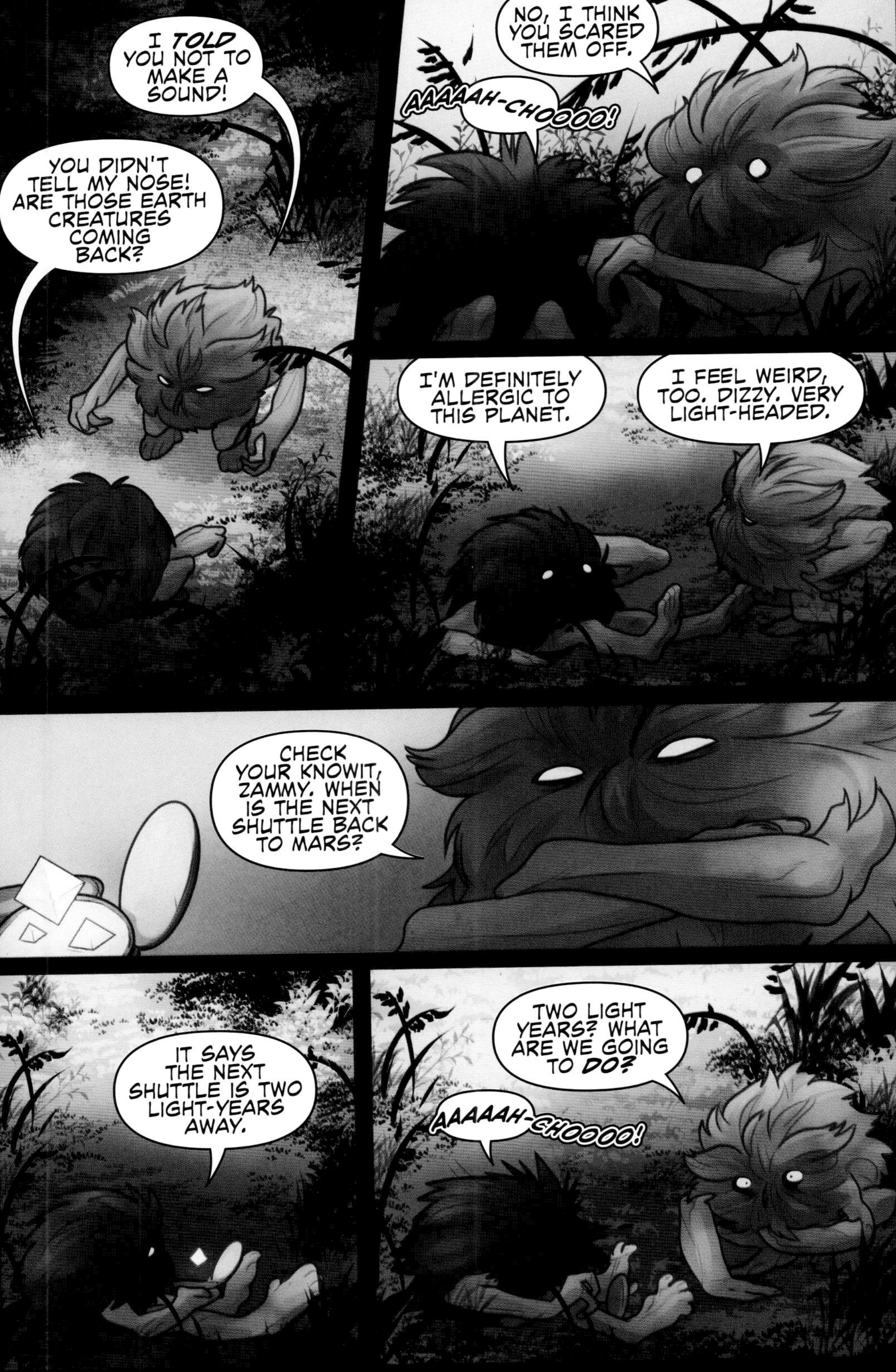
I TOLD YOU NOT TO MAKE A SOUND!
YOU DIDN'T TELL MY NOSE! ARE THOSE EARTH CREATURES COMING BACK?
NO, I THINK YOU SCARED THEM OFF.
AAAAAH-CHOOOO!
I'M DEFINITELY ALLERGIC TO THIS PLANET.
I FEEL WEIRD, TOO. DIZZY. VERY LIGHT-HEADED.
CHECK YOUR KNOWIT, ZAMMY. WHEN IS THE NEXT SHUTTLE BACK TO MARS?
IT SAYS THE NEXT SHUTTLE IS TWO LIGHT-YEARS AWAY.
TWO LIGHT YEARS? WHAT ARE WE GOING TO DO?
AAAAAH-CHOOOO!

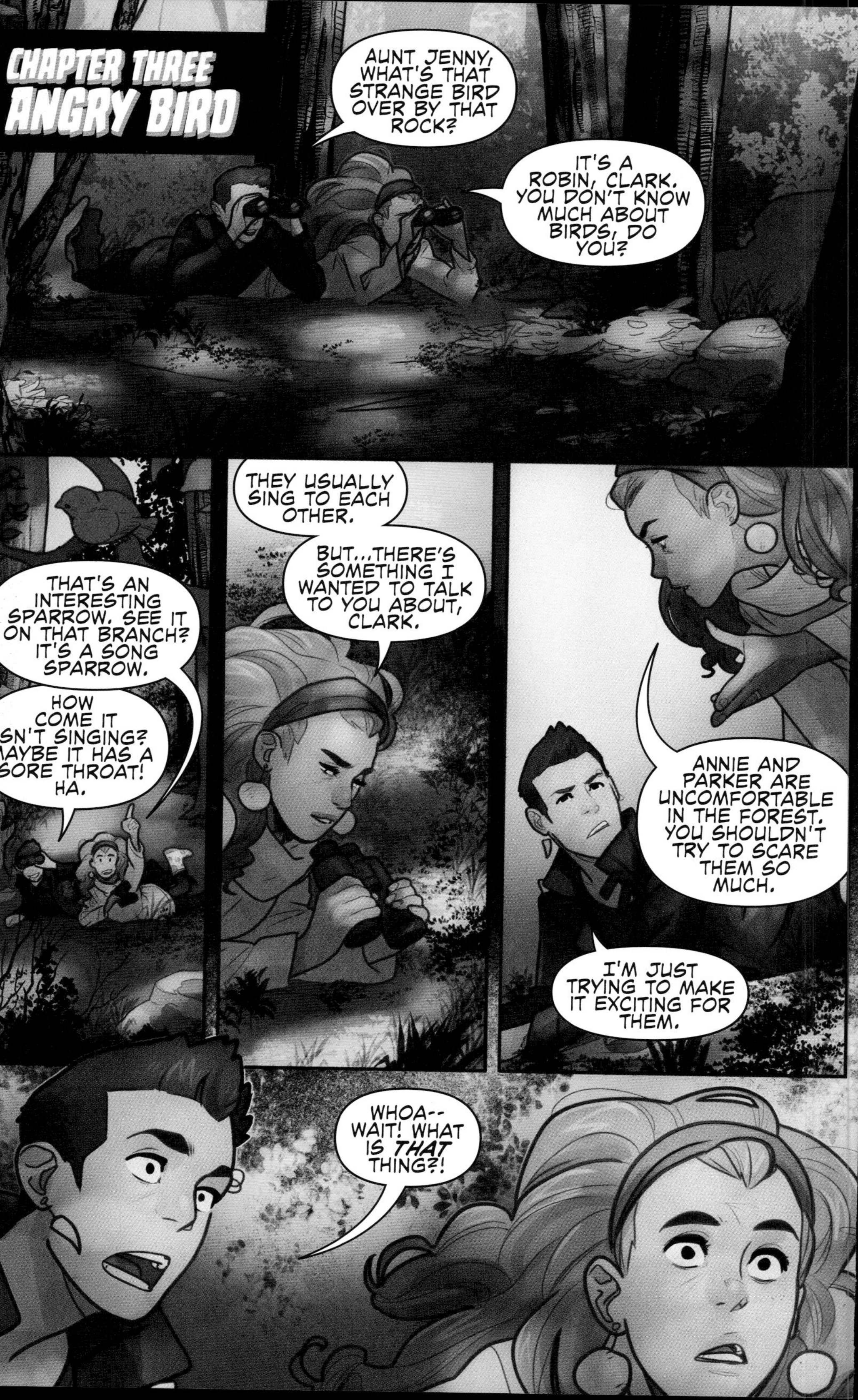
CHAPTER THREE
ANGRY BIRD
AUNT JENNY, WHAT'S THAT STRANGE BIRD OVER BY THAT ROCK?
IT'S A ROBIN, CLARK. YOU DON'T KNOW MUCH ABOUT BIRDS, DO YOU?
THAT'S AN INTERESTING SPARROW. SEE IT ON THAT BRANCH? IT'S A SONG SPARROW.
HOW COME IT SN'T SINGING? MAYBE IT HAS A SORE THROAT! HA.
THEY USUALLY SING TO EACH OTHER.
BUT...THERE'S SOMETHING I WANTED TO TALK TO YOU ABOUT, CLARK.
ANNIE AND PARKER ARE UNCOMFORTABLE IN THE FOREST. YOU SHOULDN'T TRY TO SCARE THEM SO MUCH.
I'M JUST TRYING TO MAKE IT EXCITING FOR THEM.
WHOA-- WAIT! WHAT IS *THAT* THING?!

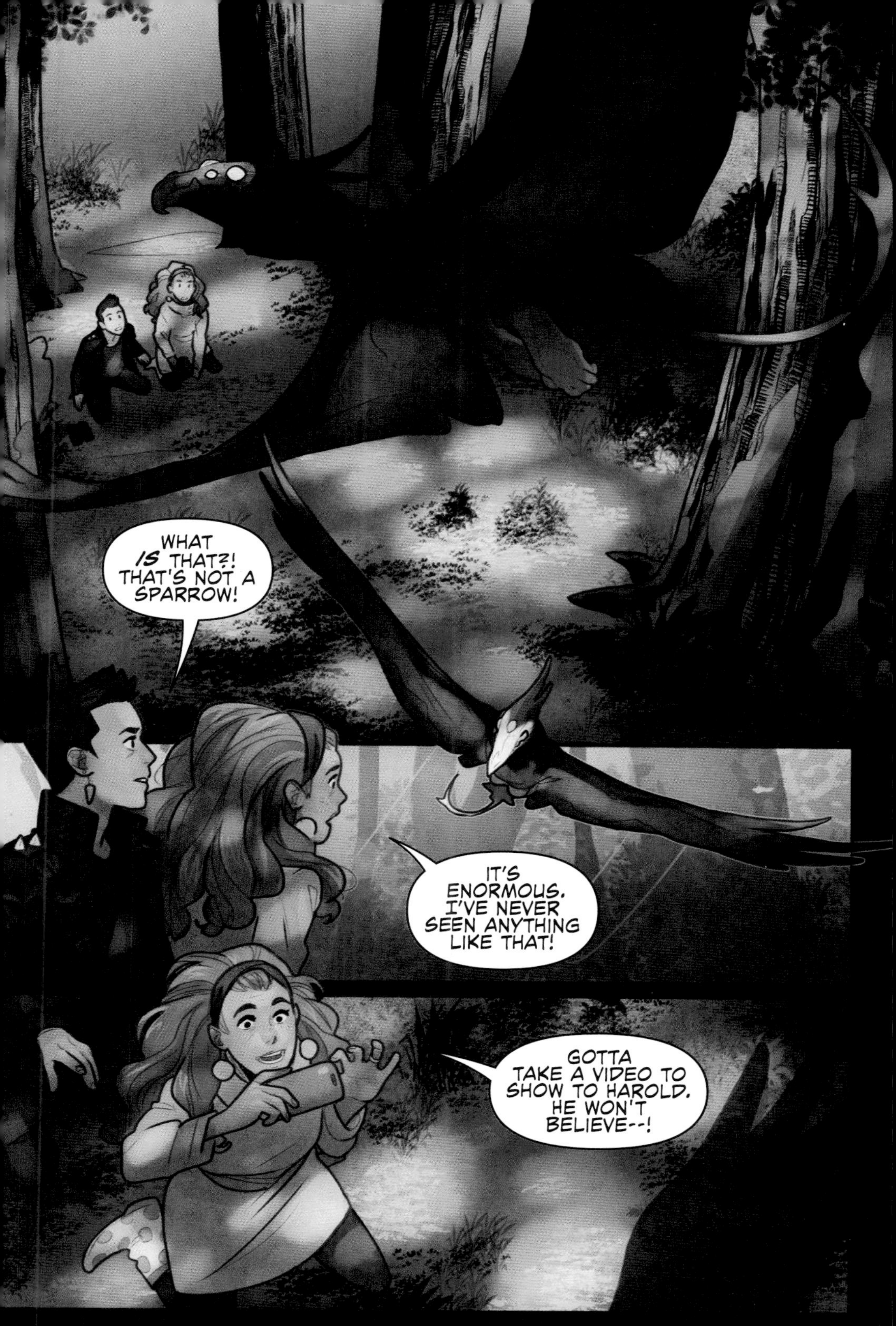
WHAT *IS* THAT?! THAT'S NOT A SPARROW!
IT'S ENORMOUS. I'VE NEVER SEEN ANYTHING LIKE THAT!
GOTTA TAKE A VIDEO TO SHOW TO HAROLD. HE WON'T BELIEVE--!

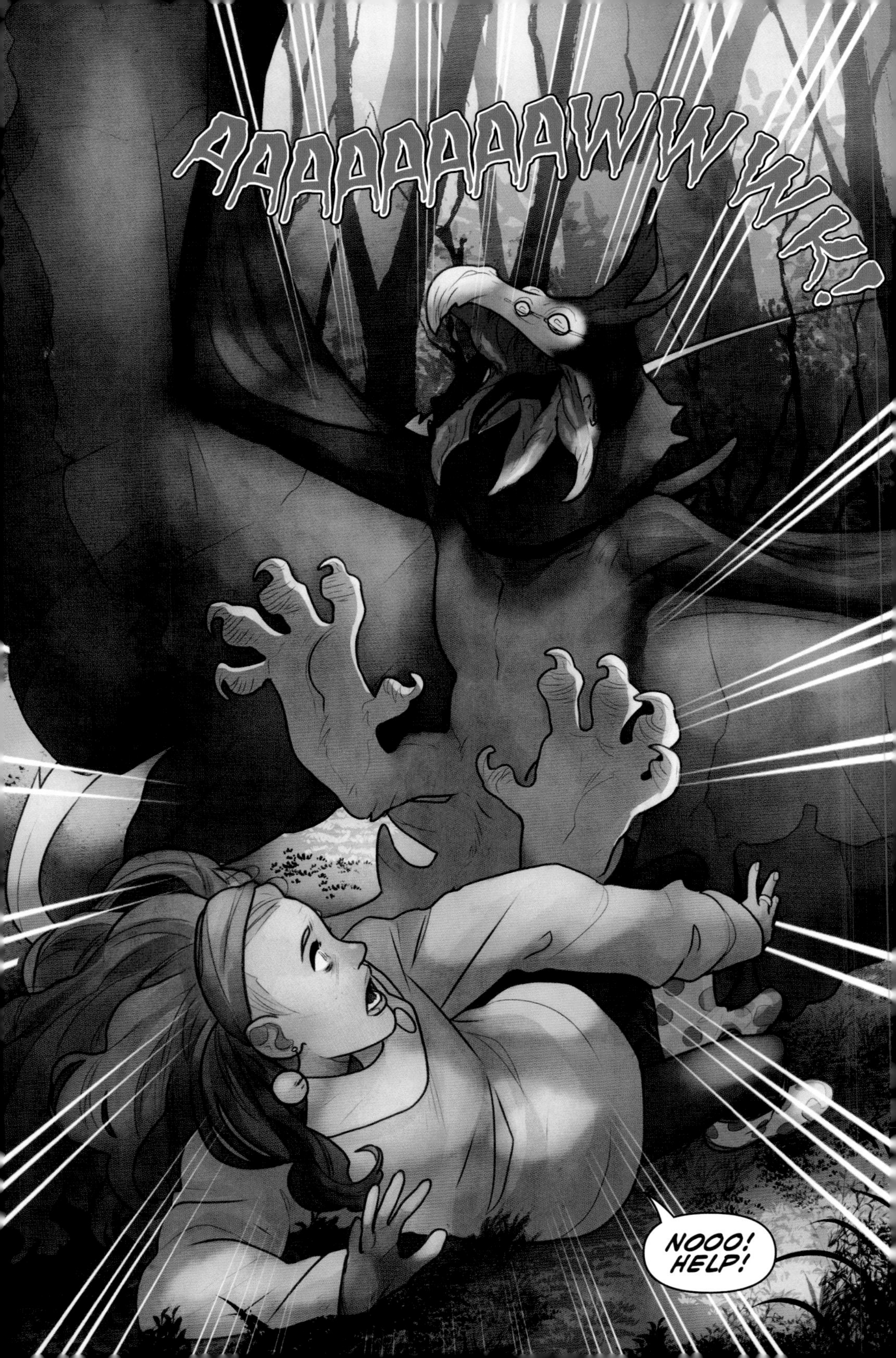
AAAAAAAAAWWWK!!
NOOO! HELP!

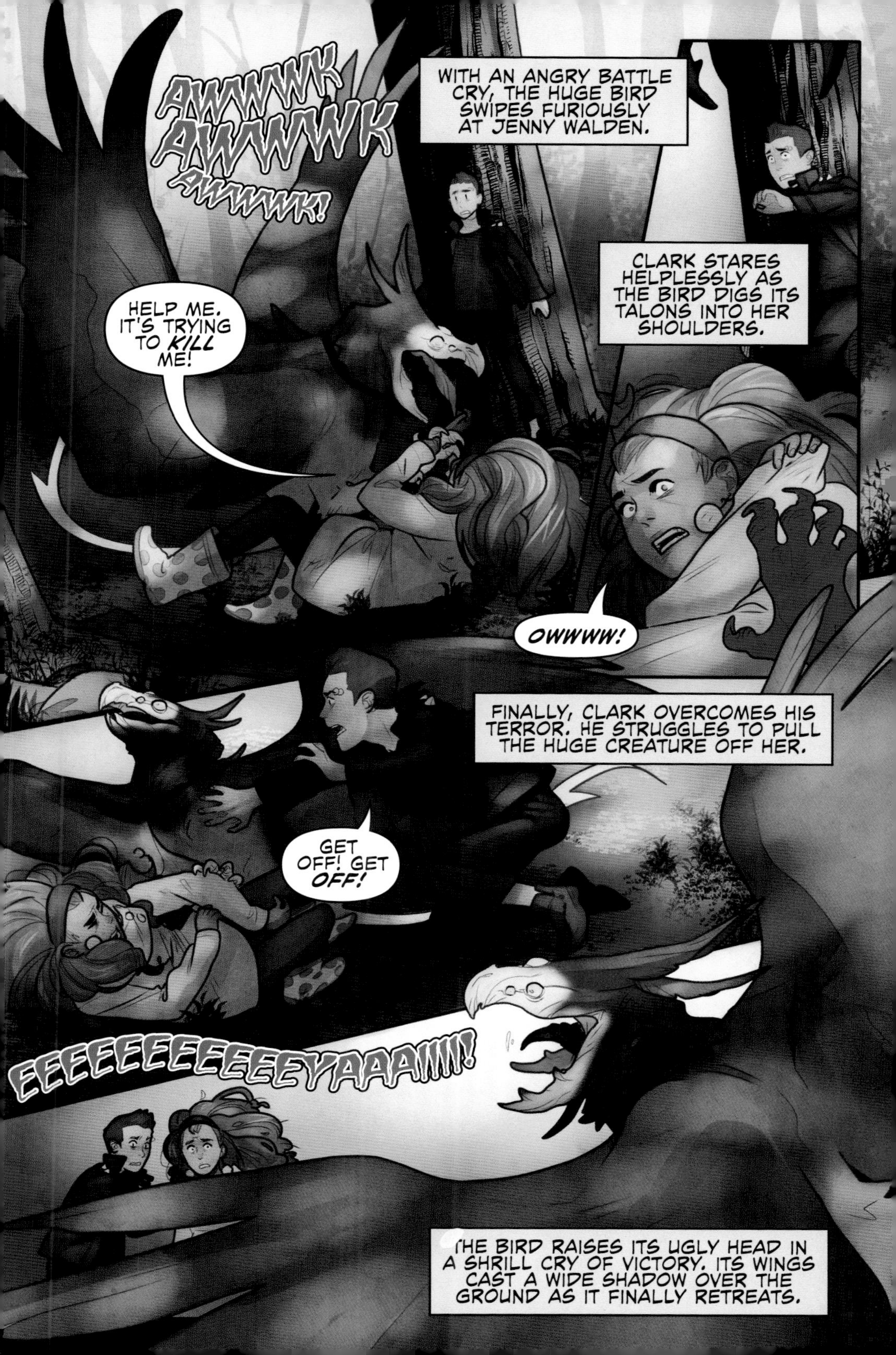
AWWWWK AWWWWK AWWWWK!
WITH AN ANGRY BATTLE CRY, THE HUGE BIRD SWIPES FURIOUSLY AT JENNY WALDEN.
HELP ME. IT'S TRYING TO KILL ME!
CLARK STARES HELPLESSLY AS THE BIRD DIGS ITS TALONS INTO HER SHOULDERS.
OWWWW!
FINALLY, CLARK OVERCOMES HIS TERROR. HE STRUGGLES TO PULL THE HUGE CREATURE OFF HER.
GET OFF! GET OFF!
EEEEEEEEEEEEEYAAAIIIII!
THE BIRD RAISES ITS UGLY HEAD IN A SHRILL CRY OF VICTORY. ITS WINGS CAST A WIDE SHADOW OVER THE GROUND AS IT FINALLY RETREATS.

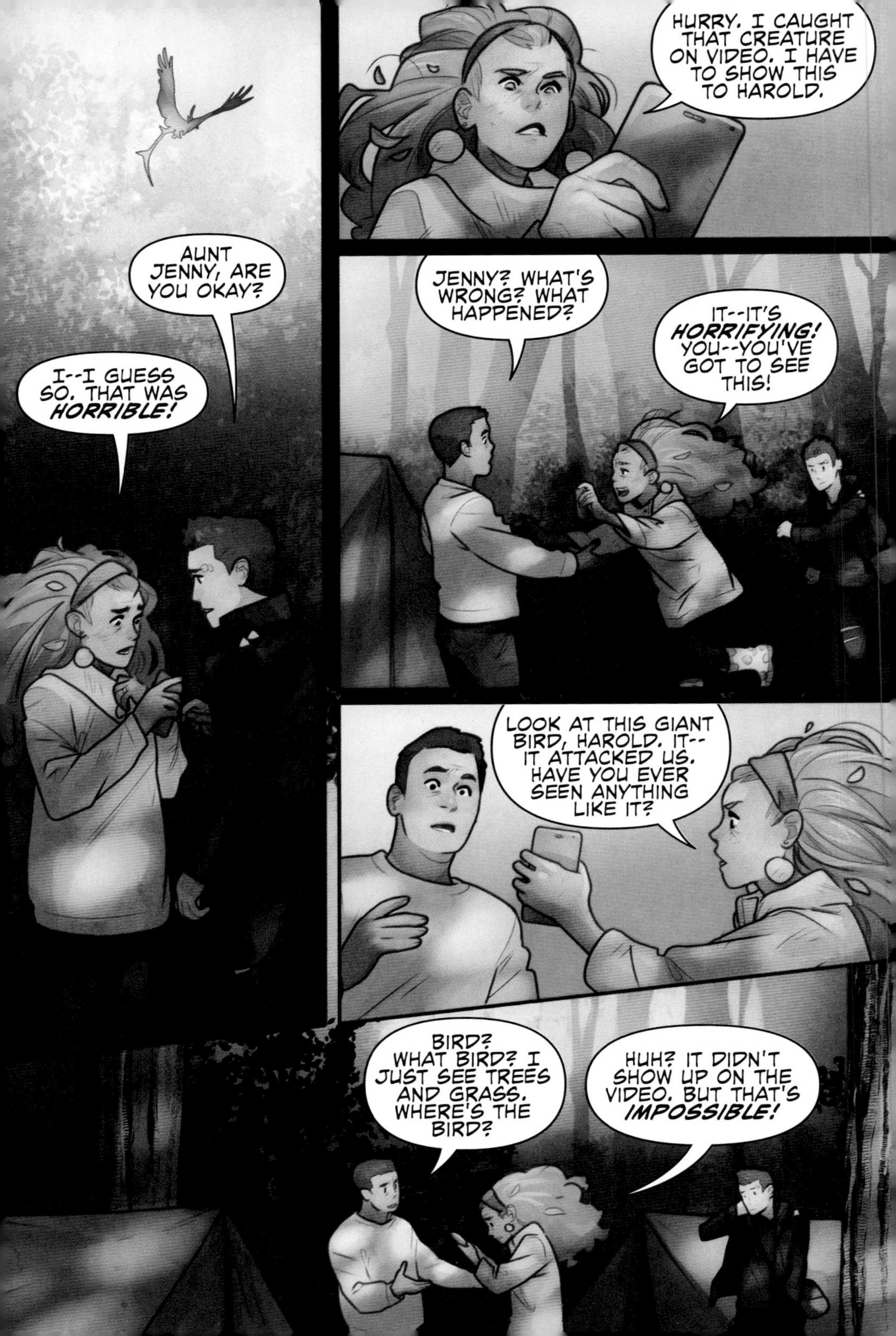
AUNT JENNY, ARE YOU OKAY?
I--I GUESS SO. THAT WAS *HORRIBLE!*
HURRY. I CAUGHT THAT CREATURE ON VIDEO. I HAVE TO SHOW THIS TO HAROLD.
JENNY? WHAT'S WRONG? WHAT HAPPENED?
IT--IT'S *HORRIFYING!* YOU--YOU'VE GOT TO SEE THIS!
LOOK AT THIS GIANT BIRD, HAROLD. IT--IT ATTACKED US. HAVE YOU EVER SEEN ANYTHING LIKE IT?
BIRD? WHAT BIRD? I JUST SEE TREES AND GRASS. WHERE'S THE BIRD?
HUH? IT DIDN'T SHOW UP ON THE VIDEO. BUT THAT'S *IMPOSSIBLE!*

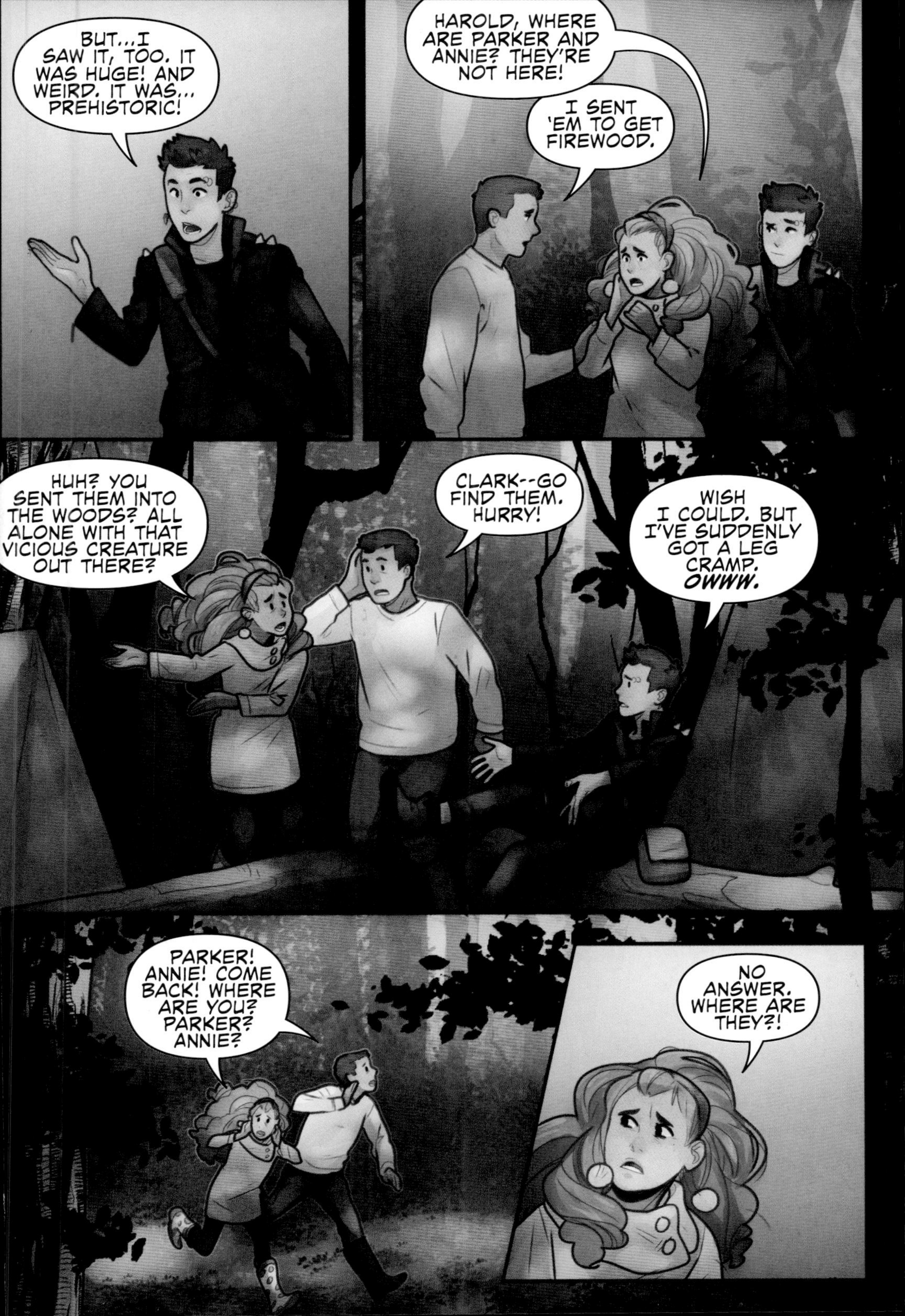
BUT...I SAW IT, TOO. IT WAS HUGE! AND WEIRD. IT WAS... PREHISTORIC!
HAROLD, WHERE ARE PARKER AND ANNIE? THEY'RE NOT HERE!
I SENT 'EM TO GET FIREWOOD.
HUH? YOU SENT THEM INTO THE WOODS? ALL ALONE WITH THAT VICIOUS CREATURE OUT THERE?
CLARK--GO FIND THEM. HURRY!
WISH I COULD. BUT I'VE SUDDENLY GOT A LEG CRAMP. OWWW.
PARKER! ANNIE! COME BACK! WHERE ARE YOU? PARKER? ANNIE?
NO ANSWER. WHERE ARE THEY?!

# JUST BEYOND™

## COLLECT THEM ALL!

### Set of 4 Hardcover Books ISBN: 978-1-5321-4754-8

New York Times Bestselling Author
**R.L. STINE**
**JUST BEYOND**
Illustrated by KELLY & NICHOLE MATTHEWS

HAPPY LANDINGS
Nature Preserve

VOLUME 5:
THE HORROR AT HAPPY LANDINGS

**Hardcover Book ISBN**
**978-1-5321-4755-5**

New York Times Bestselling Author
**R.L. STINE**
**JUST BEYOND**
Illustrated by KELLY & NICHOLE MATTHEWS

VOLUME 6: POSSESSED AGAIN

**Hardcover Book ISBN**
**978-1-5321-4756-2**

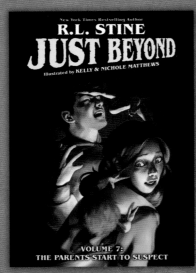

New York Times Bestselling Author
**R.L. STINE**
**JUST BEYOND**
Illustrated by KELLY & NICHOLE MATTHEWS

VOLUME 7:
THE PARENTS START TO SUSPECT

**Hardcover Book ISBN**
**978-1-5321-4757-9**

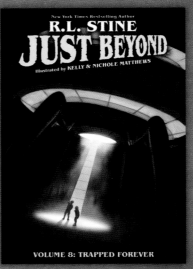

New York Times Bestselling Author
**R.L. STINE**
**JUST BEYOND**
Illustrated by KELLY & NICHOLE MATTHEWS

VOLUME 8: TRAPPED FOREVER

**Hardcover Book ISBN**
**978-1-5321-4758-6**